LITERATI PRESS
COMICS LP NOVELS
PUBLISHING COMPANY

·····IN ASSOCIATION WITH THE·····

BA AC

·····PRESENTS·····

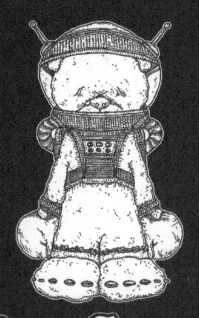

THE STORY
of
IVAN A. ALEXANDER
-IVAN THE INNOCENCE-

THE STORY
of
IVAN A. ALEXANDER
-IVAN THE INNOCENCE-

Awakened from slumber, Ivan is disoriented.

Unfamiliar sounds flutter, like vampire bats, throughout his private chambers.

An imposing geometric structure has been situated upon the periphery of his asylum. Emboldened by curiosity, he delicately steps inside.

Where he is quickly met with a well-timed, though poorly thrown, right cross. It is, however, powerful enough to dislodge his bothersome bottom left-wise molar.

The pain of which had occupied his entire previous evening.

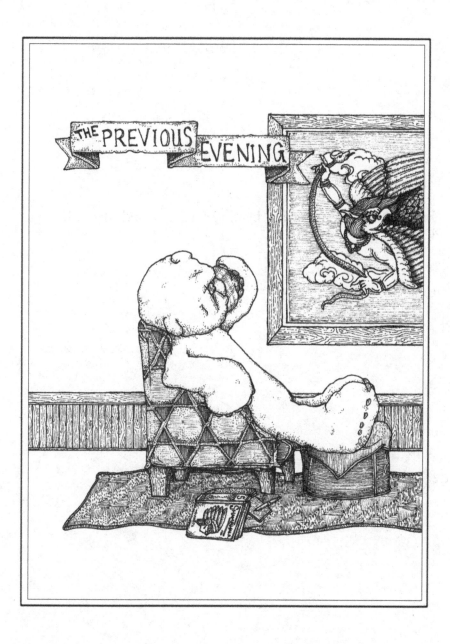

Incidentally, the following beating forces all sight from his left eye.

Saddened by confusion and thusly confused even further by this sadness, Ivan is alone. An objective presence ominously reveals itself.

Only to immediately complicate Ivan's standing in this sensitive brave new world further still.

As for needs and wants, one can usually find anything early on a Saturday at a Morning-Market.

Some things are subject to intense speculation while others may be simultaneously overlooked. An exchange of considerable suspicion is made.

Familiarity with the fundamental laws of the universe can lead to exciting, albeit quite dubious, new possibilities.

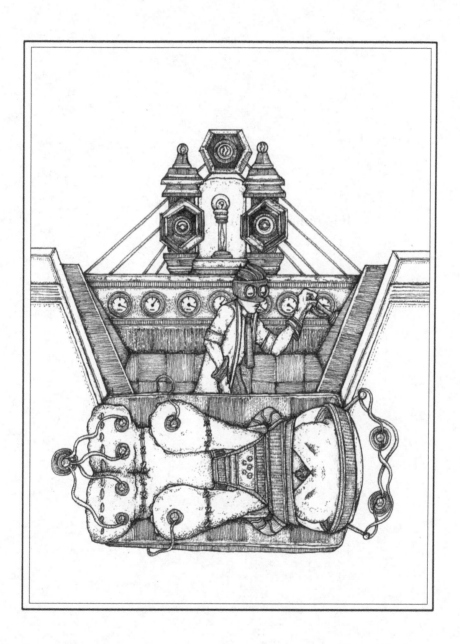

Re-animated, Ivan kills a man.

And then for a brief thoroughly intense moment, with the pull of blood still fresh on his heightened senses, he contemplates killing every man he sees.

He immediately retreats to the solitude and shelter of what is left of his forest.

Where he quietly discovers that an oxygenated mobility-suit can sometimes double as an explorative jet-pack.

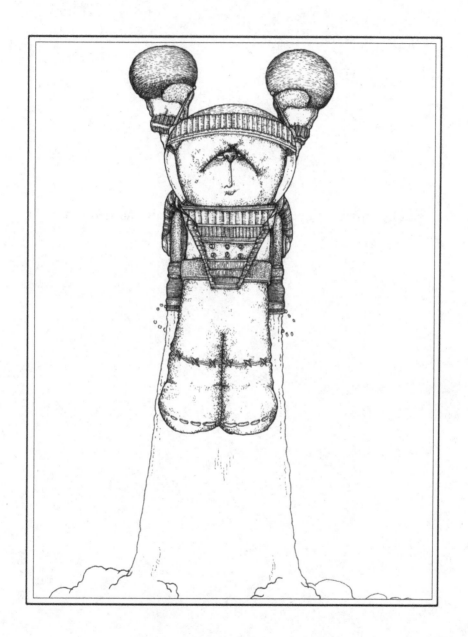

But he only ever gains half of what he truly needed.

Epilogue

Fin.

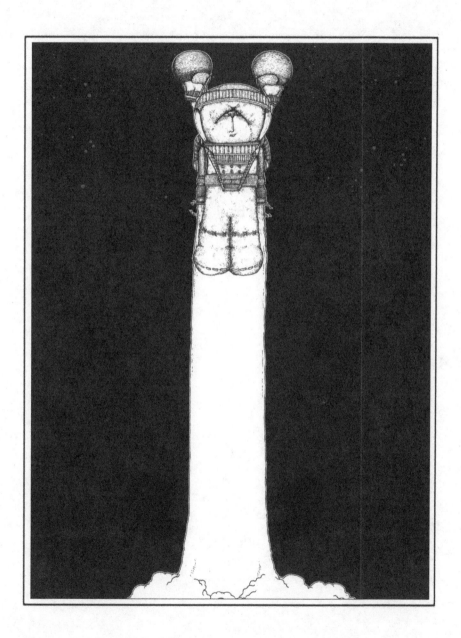

Thank You.

the BLOODIED PAST
of
JINGLE HEIMER S.V.S.

the Bloodied Past
of
Jingle Heimer S.V.S.

The morning air was crisp with promise when Jingle sensed he almost heard something.

Abruptly, he sensed only suffocating regret.

He could not breathe. He couldn't move. He could neither think nor imagine. He began to despair.

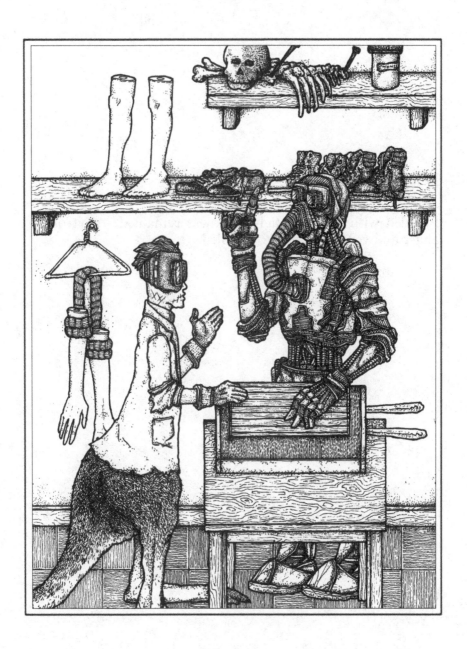

Flooded with light, an ugly darkness remained. A pit of anger and vengeance had to be filled.

Vengeance is the long con of the ego. It is berating, mindless crows echoing self-doubt and unyielding to any point of a rationale.

Anger comes easy, like a gift from an over-accommodating beast helping you down the stairs and into the pit.

Which must then, of course, be filled with blood.

An inevitable silence full of introspection would closely follow. An objective personal inventory would be taken.

Jingle began to contemplate the boiled skulls piled along the brick wall adjacent to the dining room.

Where, incidentally, he climbed for a post-dinner respite.

As he dreamed, the terror and folly of his actions were aggressively revealed to him.

Thus, awakening to the full potential of reality was arousing. Plans to leave were hastily made.

He prepared a platter of cuccumber sandwiches, but did not bother taking any. Instead, he left a folded note inside the empty jar of mayonnaise.

He felt that he had arrived at a crossroads where he could peacefully perpetuate happiness to anonymous passers-by.

But, there was no one to ever give it to.

So, he just let it go.

Epilogue

Fin.

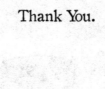

Thank You.